Out of Time in Wan Chai

The writer, Fan Tong, is a journalist
based in Hong Kong and reporting
about China for several French
professionnal magazines.

He has published several crime novels,
all taking place in China. *Out of Time
in Wan Chai* is his first work
translated in English,
as well as in Swedish.

FAN TONG

CHINA BLACK

Non-action Press

Original title :
Voguant vers l'avenir lumineux
(Sailing towards the bright future ahead)

Translated from the French
by Marie-Hélène Arnauld
and Denis Williamson

1st edition:
2012, Blue Lettuce Publishing, Hong Kong

This edition:
Copyright © 2014, Non-action Press
(Éditions du non-agir, Paris)

Illustrations:
Picture of a tramway in Hong-Kong is © François Boucher.
Hong Kong night "skyline" is © Samuel Louis (Base64) & Carol
Spears, modified and reproduced under the *Creative Commons
Attribution-Share Alike 3.0 Unported* licence.
The Red Guard dancer comes from a propaganda poster
from the Cultural Revolution in China.

ISBN 979-10-92475-20-3

我们应当把世界进步的情况和光明
的前途，常常向人民宣传，
使人民建立起胜利的信心

We should carry on constant propaganda
among the people on the facts of world
progress and the bright future ahead
so that they will build their
confidence in victory.

« On the Chungking negotiations »
(*October 17, 1945*),
Selected works of Mao Tse-Tung, volume IV.

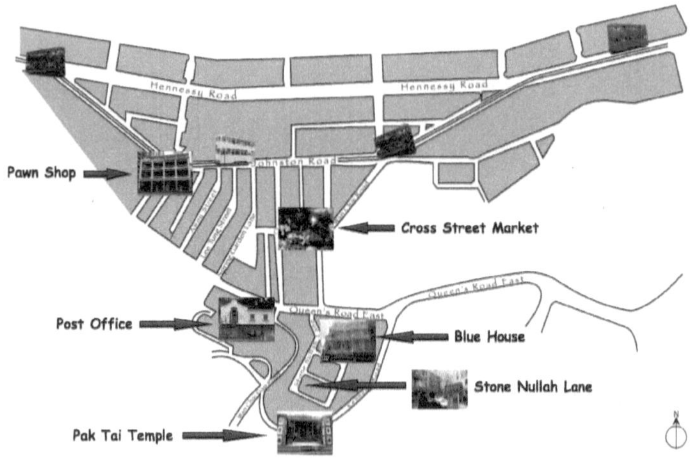

Wan Chai district, Hong Kong island

Chapter 1

I N MY DREAM a flower blooms, a tiny wild flower. So tiny I can hardly see it, a scent so subtle I can hardly smell it. And yet, when I wake, it is the only thing I remember.

Every morning a girl in her *qipao* smiles at him and dances, a cigarette between her lips. Ever since he put her poster on the wall opposite his bed.

God! Ten past eight already. Lethargic because of the air con churning away in the corner of his window, he stretched and wondered why his alarm clock hadn't gone off, until he remembered Valiant Heart, number 9 in the fifth at Happy Valley the night before. At three to one, he hadn't made a fortune but it was nice all the same. There it is, stupid, the whole racing programme from last night, on your chair. In big letters: 13th of July.

So today is the 14th, French national day and a holiday. That's why he hadn't set his alarm. The 14th of July... the parades on the red hot avenues of Haiphong or Hanoi... "From the steel grey skies they are falling in their hundreds, the red berets who dare and who win..." Tch tch. He hadn't won much, just the right to die, years later, in his bed or in the street, of a stroke or a heart attack, just like anybody else.

Watch your cholesterol, Monsieur Chambon...

He got up and stumbled past the smoker, a present from Martin Mack, a regular at the race course who, when he needed the money, occasionally did a bit of door to door for Lucky Strike. Damp and badly stained, the poor girl looked more and more like an icon in the fight against cancer. She had been hanging there for less than two months... This damned humidity! Tomorrow, get rid of her. Having said that, his wardrobe was in an even worse state; a nursery for mushrooms, a tropical cellar for Roquefort. To wear nothing but polyester; it makes one's skin itchy but at least it doesn't rot.

His bathroom already felt like a sauna. The inevitable cockroach fled into the air vent. Cold shower, energetic scrub, teeth and shave... Music, suddenly. A neighbour's radio, next door or below. The latest hit of Anita Mui the queen of canto pop, announced the loud speaker.

The lyrics didn't mean anything, Cantonese was like double Dutch to him, but the tune didn't displease him. His blade cut a neat line through the white foam spread on his cheek and, for a brief instant, he was back by the Red River cutting through the mountains of Tonkin.

Oh shit! The phone.

He pretended not to hear and steadfastly attacked the stubble on his Adam's apple. They'll soon tire and hang up. But no, they persisted, someone who must have known he was at home, was even annoyed perhaps by his lack of response. It's all instant gratification nowadays. He went and picked up the phone.

"Hello, is that Roger Chambon?"

"Yes."

"It's Lavinier... Tell me, you are coming for drinks at the Consulate, aren't you?"

He confirmed with a grunt, which didn't put off his caller.

"Must talk to you about some business... We can discuss it there, all right?"

New grunt, but begrudgingly affirmative. Some business, here we go again... With tips from Captain Lavinier, the military attaché, one had had to be careful. Nine times out of ten they led nowhere.

Chapter 2

JOHNNY KWOK FINISHED his noodles, put down his chopsticks, forming a poor man's bridge over his bowl, and found himself staring at the top of the wig of the middle aged man who was sharing his table, and wolfing down his noodle soup like a pig its fodder.

Johnny exhaled heavily in the direction of the synthetic mane, just to see if it was properly stuck on. The man looked up. Seeing Johnny's ironic smile, he shrugged his shoulders and wolfed even faster. Johnny immediately forgot about him and his attention turned elsewhere: the table of workers producing more smoke than an Indonesian volcano, the bank clerks wearing thick glasses and sprinting through their food, the old guys picking at their plates of tripe, the waitress with her fat bum forcing her way with difficulty through the middle of all these, and the foul-mouthed woman cashier near the door.

The pointless scurrying around of the different human groups always amazed him. Like that of his little lads, whose illusions were already lost. His little lads or his punks or wankers, his arse-holes, his runts, his wretched ones, his nuisances, his lobotomies, his ugly spotty faces, his little pricks, his rat faces, his tofu fuckers and even more permutations of the basic elements of foul language. The deplorable permutations: the wankers of lizard's pricks; the redundant ones: arse-hole of a tofu fucker; the multi-handicapped ones: spotty rat-faced lobotomies; and last but not least, the most-abundant polysemic ones as difficult to recite as a verse of *The Peony Pavilion* and as complex to predict as the twists and turns of a Louis Cha novel. This is how police inspector Johnny Kwok was inspired to describe this group (whilst his ordinarily sombre imagination grew darker the moment he thought of them) hovering on the fringe of the population of the colony which his superiors had ordered him to watch in these troubled times: college kids and school kids.

"With your cool and your empathy, you'll soon make friends with them."

Johnny had not in the least taken as a compliment his chief's justification for volunteering him. On the contrary, every time he looked at himself in the mirror it was to check that he did not look either cool or empathetic. Argh…!!!

But a job was a job. He had to acquit himself honourably and keep a close eye on these fools who, under the cover of their Committee of Patriotic Schools – my arse – demanded the abolition of the thirteen decrees which the fascist, colonial government had passed to establish its brainwashing education programme. These excitable kids (aping the Red Guards of the cultural revolution who, over the border, were ransacking China) had been constantly demonstrating since the beginning of May, declaiming endlessly from Mao's *Little Red Book*. They threw stones at the riot police, set fire to letter boxes and cars, and would do a lot more harm if no one stopped them. Schools had been closed, teachers and even kids had been arrested... a few weeks behind bars would teach these savages a few lessons about life. A few kicks in the arse and a bit of ill-treatment, even better! He and a colleague had grabbed two of them the day before, who were sticking up posters calling for the kidnapping of the Governor. Whoosh! Straight to Pokfulam prison where, with the screws, they had had a bit of fun with them. A bowl of tea with hair floating on it, as an appetizer just to tickle their throats, and then strip off! Thorough search in case they had hidden the complete works of Mao in their underpants. Pity they were not girls, these little puftas. The operation of the following day was more promising in that respect.

Johnny got up from the table, paid for his meal and stepped out of the Lung Mun Restaurant, his local. Outside, the sun was melting Johnston Road. Vehicles and pedestrians moved slowly and he would not have been surprised to see one or two of them being swallowed up by the tarmac.

The adjacent building, China Products, still bore the marks of the recent police offensive: doors smashed in, broken windows and the walls streaked with soot from a fire. No doubt about it the Maoist bandits who had occupied it had suffered a heavy defeat.

A tram went past, unnoticed by everyone else. Johnny tensed up: always be suspicious of calm waters and warm ashes.

Chapter 3

AT THE CONSUL'S no one pushes, everyone remains courteous and cordial under the portrait of President Mitterrand, nevertheless there's a bit of a bottleneck, and the white table cloth of the buffet does not stay white for very long.

Chambon, wisely, has anticipated the situation. Just before the opening of the buffet, he winked at a waiter who brought him a glass of champagne and a plate of appetizers, then settled in a corner, next to a small table where he placed them. Being naturally shy and with a feeling of not really belonging, he always stands to one side at official receptions. He doesn't join in the conversations and very seldom does anybody talk to him. He doesn't mind and accepts being thought of as boring with his uncouth face, his wrestler's physique, his country-squire suits, his after-shave and his ties with the ageing patterns he had bought some twenty odd years ago in Catinat street in Saigon. He doesn't like shopping and knows he has the imagination of a Neanderthal. It's a bit like at the club where he occasionally goes. Pastis they don't have, so what can he order apart from a beer or a whisky?

His injury, his missing hand, puts people off too. They ask about it behind his back, he knows that.

They are embarrassed by the explanation: "A grenade, in Indochina. Dien Bien Phu, I think..."

Double mistake. Not a grenade but a mortar shell and not Dien Bien Phu but the Black River, two years previously. Big difference for those who were there, but he doesn't correct them, why bother? Nothing to be gained.

Rumours abound also, of course, about his profession and his company, SCOMDEF. They don't help.

His is an unrewarding job. Discretion is key. One gets used to it. It's enough to follow a few rules of common sense and watch what you say. With some contacts however, this game can make one paranoid: dealing with them becomes exhausting. Apart from that, business lunches, business seminars, business trips, most of them are unproductive. Days, weeks, months of shaking hands, exchanging name cards, following tip-offs. Even when they lead somewhere, it's no more exciting than selling vacuum cleaners. He knows this for sure. He compared it with Jean, his cousin who does actually sell Hoovers in Orleans. Is he bored? He could philosophize, but people would think that he was getting out of his depth, so he would say no, the days do not drag, they are just empty. He lives in a perpetual present without milestones, highlights or memories, a waking hibernation, like a bear on the moon.

So Hong Kong is not exciting?

Chambon hated to disillusion his occasional visitors, usually he just sighed at their fantasies. Take the commercial manager of the factory in Tulle, for example, who visited a month ago. On the morning of his arrival, he was already excited at the idea of going around the bars in Wan Chai one evening.

"Lockhart Road, you must know..."

"Er... yeah..."

"They recommend it in here."

'Here' was a little dog-eared booklet with a picture on the cover showing a topless lady serving a G & T to a tourist: *Hong Kong Bachelor's Guide*. This guy had pulled it out of his pocket, his eyes alight.

But 'bachelor' means being single, and...

That's why Chambon had declined to join in the expedition to the road in question which, it's true, he had visited in the past but which now he found somewhat distasteful. He was not made of wood of course, yet his physical needs – he didn't talk of love any longer – he satisfied with Jenny, a not so young woman, not pretty anymore, who worked Java Road, in North Point, almost a slum, two hundred and fifty per cent Chinese. With a wink and a provocative smile she had attracted him as he wandered in that area one day. A red heart decorated the door of her small pink flat where the bed squeaked like a rusted expeditionary forces' half-track after rains. He had tried to make her understand that it didn't help his concentration. Waste of time, she had not changed it. Sordid maybe, but no more so than Lockhart Road which stank of sad and cowardly virility and only a more cosmopolitan air of misfortune. At least, Jenny was a nice person. Sometimes he brought her flowers, to keep up the illusion. She was touched and amused at the same time by his kindness.

From where he was standing, he could observe Lavinier, graduate of Saint-Cyr with the permanent suntan of a beach-boy, absorbed in a conversation about sports. These gentlemen, four or five of them, were assessing France's chances at the Olympics, at the end of the month. The military attaché, a fan of cycling, was adamant that 'our cyclists' could do it. Morelon was coaching the team, no small potato. The others expressed their scepticism, even scorn: "Cycling, drugs and all the rest, their medals? No thank you. Fencing, on the other hand, or horse riding, that's more honest, well, I hope so, who knows, but for the rest, the wooden spoon..."

Captain Lavinier, losing interest and running out of things to say caught Chambon's eye. A cautious though rather theatrical gesture pointed in the direction of the garden of the residence. A polite conversation, five minutes later, under a bauhinia tree:

"Delighted to see you."
"And I you."
"How are you?"
"Well, and you?"
"Your wife and children?"
"Back in France for the holidays."
"Whereabouts?"
"Royan."
"A nice town."
"Peaceful, above all. How is business?"

In any business you need demand but the world was on such a course that there was no risk of that decreasing soon, as long as people could pay.

Unfortunately, the latter posed something of a problem, these days.

"I can guarantee that the financial soundness of the project I am about to propose to you is cast in bronze."

Chambon smiled to himself. For the twenty-five years he had been in this profession, this kind of introduction meant that there was almost certainly a snag.

To this Lavinier objected: "No, I assure you, although I won't hide anything from you. It is about a Chinese job, but the other one, Taiwan actually."

Taiwan, he must be joking. This was not merely a snag but a rip.

"The client is inviting us for dinner tomorrow evening. You are available, I take it?"

Paris had already given the green light provisionally, continued the military attaché. On condition, naturally, of total secrecy. At the slightest indiscretion, the authorities would deny all knowledge, and the contractor would be on his own.

Chambon ran his fingers through his hair. Snag... rip... more like torn to shreds.

Chapter 4

THE STREET LIGHTS, lit at only half mast, conferred an air of gloom onto Johnston Road, and Siu Fung had the impression that she was waiting for a funeral. Yet the dim light, in a way, reassured her.

At last, the tram emerged from Queensway. It slowly passed the Methodist church and the old pawn shop, rattling along lines which, each time she saw them, she thought were too narrow for its high body: wasn't it going to topple over?

She screwed up her eyes to read its number: 88, and its destination: Causeway Bay. The very tram she had to take. It reached her and stopped. On its side an advert praised the merits of Campbell's tomato soup. She took a deep breath and got on.

As planned, Yeung Tak was already on board, downstairs, sitting not too far behind the driver. He saw her too but they pretended not to know each other: also planned. She clambered upstairs, bought her ticket from the conductor and sat right at the front, with her satchel secure between her legs.

As she had hoped, there were not many passengers. Who would risk being caught in the street at curfew, now less than an hour and a half away? And even more, who wanted to be an accomplice to the odious strategy of the transport companies which claimed to keep their service going, but only by replacing striking employees with scabs? Not that they were finding it easy to do, fortunately; hadn't she waited a good twenty minutes before getting a tram?

*

With its roughcast wall outside, and its rustic furniture inside, the French restaurant in Happy Valley to which the Taiwanese had invited the two men was trying to imitate a French provincial style. The question was, which one?

Lavinier made the introductions. Mr Kuang occupied an important position in the National Centre for Strategic Studies in Taipei.

"You have before you a perfect francophone and Francophile," added the captain.

The person in question, a fragile gnome with a baby face, held out a tiny frail hand that Chambon was scared he might crush, and explained the captain was referring to a period in his life now long gone alas, namely his youth, when he was studying in Paris.

Chambon pretended to sympathize. Youth was a gift that everyone loses eventually. Not worth getting all worked up about: no big deal. Drinks were ordered, glasses were raised then Kuang introduced his whatever-it-was-called Centre; a respectable academic institute where foreign hosts were regularly invited to exchange ideas, in a friendly atmosphere.

"We would be happy to welcome you."

"I am not a very good speaker."

Both true and false: Chambon rarely strung more than six words together at a time, yet, in his profession, this constituted an asset...

Starters. The conversation continued in a courteous manner. One talked of polemology in general: the evolution of strategic doctrines and new technologies applied to the industries of defence.

Main course. *Entrecôte marchand de vin* for everybody. One took as examples various theatres of war all over the world, working subtly towards Asia.

Cheese, dessert, coffee? No, yes, why not? One mentioned certain types of equipment useful in tense situations: ground to air missiles in particular.

Liqueur...

Chapter 5

THE TRAM PASSED Gilman's garage at the corner of Johnston and Hennessy roads, and sped off towards Causeway Bay. Everything was quiet and Siu Fung told herself to be calm. Such strange ideas one has at times, she would have liked to listen to some music to lighten her journey. The Reynettes for instance, or even better the Beatles. Pure products of capitalism they were, tickets to their concerts at the Princess Theatre had been obscenely expensive – only the rich kids had been able to buy them – but one had to admit that the great global dialectic often produced some rather enticing contradictions. Well, she didn't really know, she hadn't gone into it too deeply. Yeung Tak was firmly against foreign music, but she felt he might be wrong about this.

So, the Beatles. She would have appreciated their company, but how could it be done on a tram? Hmm, if one were to invent an electric box (and after all why not?) in which songs could be stored on tiny microgrooves, a bit like a juke-box but much smaller in size? This thing would work on a battery, one could carry it around, and there could be headphones so as not to disturb other people. In this way one could quietly appreciate one's favourite music on one's own, in the street, on the ferry or on the bus. Yes, indeed, if she could make a suggestion to the workers' association, it would be this: from now on refuse to produce the plastic flowers and other trashy objects of enslavement which come out of the factories in Hong Kong and end up in the dustbins of the whole world, and instead enforce the production of goods which are useful and attractive to the People, such as her music box.

She smiled at her reflection in the tram's window. She would mention her idea to Yeung Tak later on. Let's hope he won't laugh, as he did sometimes when she told him what was going through her mind. However... A bad smell, like burning rubber, had just reached her nostrils. Where was it coming from?

She turned around. Her gaze found the conductor, standing in the aisle, who was staring nastily at her.

"There!" he shouted, pointing a finger accusingly at her satchel.

She jumped, panic-stricken at the sight of the thin wisp of smoke coming out of it.

"A bomb!" screamed a woman passenger.

Chapter 6

THE SMOKE IS getting thicker and turning yellow. It releases an acrid smell which grips the throat. The conductor shouts even louder and everyone joins in. The tram brakes hard, with a horrible screech of metal. Siu Fung lurches into a handrail. The other passengers are falling over themselves to get out. They somehow manage to rush down the rear stairs, and scatter in the street. Several almost get run over by passing cars. The tram driver barks into his radio, calling for help, then he too quickly jumps off.

Siu Fung remains upstairs, in shock. Out of her satchel is now coming a small, white flame, mixed with the smoke, and getting bigger. At last Yeung Tak appears. He pulls her violently by the sleeve, they rush down to the door, wide open.

"Jump, quick!"

But on the other side of the road, stands a figure whom they immediately perceive as hostile. A moustache hangs on his lips, askew and far too long for his thin ferret-like face. A fake! They recognize him. He had been on the tram, but then the lip-accessory had been straight. He'd escaped with the others.

"Police! Don't move!" he barks, brandishing a gun.

Yeung Tak takes no notice and rushes into the night. A gun shot. He falls heavily onto the track. His inert body, around which is spreading a pool of red, hypnotizes Siu Fung. She wants to put her hands up, like they do in the pictures, but she doesn't manage to...

An awful noise, a burning blow in her back, the impression of being blown out of the mouth of an angry dragon, then the dull thud of her chin against the rails, the taste of blood in her mouth. New screams, the siren of a police car... She emits a cry of terror but does not hear the sound of her own voice.

Another tram, twenty or thirty metres away, at the level of Gilman's garage. It must have passed hers just before the blast. It moves away into the night. She drags herself up and starts running to catch it. A race like those in her nightmares, when she is being chased by a demon: her feet weighed down with lead, her heart and her lungs burning, however fast she runs she is not getting anywhere...

Still in her dreams, she rushes into a glass tunnel, gloomy and bright at the same time. She goes suddenly from a snail's pace to the speed of light. She is not running anymore, she is flying. The burning landscape constantly loses its shape and finds it again. She closes her eyes. When she opens them again, she has caught up with the tram.

*

She grabbed the out-stretched hand. The hand of a man, thick and rough. A foreigner's hand, white and hairy. A left hand she realized, from a certain awkwardness in the fingers catching hers. On his wrist, glittered a rather vulgar watch with a face so large, she could read the make: 'Orient', and the time: 12:30. "It can't be so late", she thought with, at the same time, a sensation of *déjà-vu*.

The musky smell of the stranger, a mixture of sweat and too much *cologne*, reminded her of the anaesthetic for her appendicitis.

And then... complete darkness.

Chapter 7

CLOTHES IN SHREDS, multiple lacerations on her arms and legs, and the characteristic smell of burning hair... Chambon formed a fairly precise idea of what could have happened to the girl, but he was far from telling anyone...

"I saw her trying to catch the tram. I helped her climb on and she literally collapsed in my arms. And then I saw these wounds. I don't know anymore than that", he told the doctor on duty.

He was returning home after his dinner with Lavinier and Kuang. They had lingered – a last cognac for the road? The Taiwanese was not anxious to go home. It must have been the last tram, almost empty. The girl was out for the count, he had sat her down on a seat and tried to warn the driver, who had not understood the situation. He almost got impatient. But he had reached his stop and remembered the hospital close by. He had taken the girl there, carrying her in his arms. Easy, she was hardly forty kilos.

No papers on her. How old could she be? Fifteen or sixteen. Undoubtedly a secondary school pupil, for she was wearing a uniform, a grey skirt and a navy blue blazer. The breast-pocket, which usually held the embroidered badge identifying the school, had unfortunately been ripped off.

"Will you pay for her hospitalization?"

Chambon mumbled an affirmative. What else could he do right now? He was asked to fill in some forms and they took two thousand five hundred dollars off him right away. Let's hope the family comes forward soon!

"You will call the police, I presume?"

The doctor nodded with a strange look, as if he had understood the question in a different way to which it had been asked.

*

White walls, white sheets, two ladies in white.

"A new Wellcome has just opened in my street. It's very convenient."

"But more expensive than the wet market."

A bottle upside down above her, a soft and transparent tube, a needle stuck into her arm, a clear liquid penetrating, drop by drop... No real pain, just a fatigue or a numbness she could not define.

She was disconcerted though. The nurses, who were busy with a patient in the next bed, had woken her up with their 'welcome'. What was that all about anyway, 'welcome'? And also, what was she doing here? The gaps in her memory took some time to fill: the tram, the bomb, Yeung Tak... but like ill-fitting pieces of a puzzle, nothing and nobody quite occupied the right place or connected with the right context. And the policeman, where did he fit in? My

God, yes! The gun shot. Yeung Tak thrown to the ground, the explosion, the flames, her mad run, and finally the foreigner, his big watch, his big hand, his strong grip... Was it him who took her to the hospital?

People were going to question her, ask her name.

"My name is Hung Kei."

She wouldn't say more: Hung Kei, the 'Red Flag'. It was Yeung Tak who had chosen it for her. She didn't want to hear about Siu Fung anymore, since she had heard that a decadent singer performing at the Ocean also bore this name.

"Hung Kei. From now on call me this", she had ordered her parents one morning.

They hadn't obeyed of course. Their choice of Siu Fung, 'Little Phoenix', unfortunately revealed the hold that romantic, liberal, middle-class ideology had on their minds. It was not their fault but, one day, they should be freed from this oppression: the correction of errors formed an essential step in any Marxist education. The task would indeed take months even years. One had to virtually start them all over again.

First of all one should rid them of the profound obscurantism deep rooted by centuries of feudalism, which had prompted them to desert their small town of Yingde, so famous for its tea, and the glorious programme of edification of communist society in China, to rush into this den of exploitation that was Hong Kong.

This desertion had brought them nothing but underpaid work: her mother as a simple dress-maker, her father a tram mechanic (the chump didn't even go on strike) and shabby accommodation: puppets of the colonial power had first crammed them together with thousands of other 'misplaced' people in a derelict camp which lacked everything and had even caught fire. Today, relocated in Lee Tung Street in Wan Chai, they had running water only once every four days and had to cook on a kerosene stove in the corridor, with the neighbours.

And to think that her mother, with the political conscience of an alga, made do when she had money worries (which was at least once a month) with a prayer to the God of the North, or even worse went begging, shamefully, a meagre sum from the charities' do-gooders, those shrews of hypocritical compassion who indulged in poor people's misfortune!

And let's not forget the serious mistake her parents had made with her: putting her in an expensive catholic school when there existed some free patriotic ones, where pupils studied just as well while learning about real life: historical and dialectical materialism, the class struggle and the thoughts of Chairman Mao.

The nurses came to take her pulse. She pretended to be asleep. A new 'welcome'... Must be a shop, since the two women had compared it with the wet market, but she had never heard of it.

On the other hand, she realized suddenly that she knew this policeman with his skewed moustache, his prying face and his eyes with their foul cruelty. He had been lurking, badly made up as a worker, outside the Transport Union meeting. And it was after this meeting that...

"Police!"

The highly pitched voice of this bastard vibrated painfully in her head. The sharp report of his gun too. He had cold-bloodedly shot at Yeung Tak. Had he killed him? Impossible!

Chapter 8

THE AMBUSH CAME as a relief...

For two days, his company had been wandering in the jungle, lost and isolated from the rest of the column, itself scattered; a big worm cut up into thirty six bloody pieces by the Viets, like bait for fishing the giant catfish.

The hunger, the thirst, the fear and, even more exhausting, the permanent nervous tension. Keeping quiet, preventing Maillard, the casualty, from screaming when he is tossed about on the stretcher, sniffing out traps... while knowing that the enemy, in a matter of hours or even minutes, will eventually find you.

Then yes, the machine-gun fire ripping through the curtain of greenery as they come down a raging torrent which will lead them to who knows where because they have lost their map and their compass, Maillard who is finished off in one burst, Astier and Campagnac who in their turn fall dead without even knowing what hit them, Sergeant Muller who yells we must take cover, but omits to say how or where, then keeps quiet for good, all of this almost brings an instant of relief.

In that instant the Comrades deploy a mortar, just

as if it were training. Chambon and his mates, caught under the sustained attack which has trapped them behind a rock, know that this one is going to be the end of them. "Hail Mary full of grace..." someone starts, Pierson maybe, before being blown into pieces.

*

He woke up one morning, feverish, lying in a dark hut that smelt of smoke. Next to him, a silent young girl prevented him from moving. From his right arm, wrapped in a bandage made of leaves, was oozing a brown smelly ointment. He understood only later that his hand was not there anymore. He also learned later that the teenager watching over him was called Thu and that she had found him in pain, by chance, on her way to the river to wash clothes.

Two months, three perhaps... he didn't have a calendar and slept all the time. His stump was healing. Recovered, or almost, there was talk in the Meo tribal village, which remained faithful to the French, of marrying him to his saviour. He hadn't really protested. He left promising to return.

The men showed him the way to a Legion outpost between the edge of the jungle and the delta. From there, someone drove him to Hanoi. A bit of hospital (the doctors stated that he had well and truly recuperated) and a lot of bureaucracy, civilian and military, for endless debriefings about his adventure. It was circuitous, never direct, but he was suspected of, he was not sure, having been taken and turned by the Viets? This happened sometimes it was said.

Eventually, the army granted him a disability pension. He left Hanoi and went to Saigon. At the bar of the Continental, he met Paul Germain, the manager of SCOMDEF, on a business trip in Asia.

Things moved quickly over a couple of pastis: "I need a person I can trust in the region. Are you tempted?"

The war ended, in Dien Bien Phu, not as expected, although somehow Chambon was not the slightest bit surprised. From his office at SCOMDEF, facing the cathedral of Saigon, he often thought about Thu. She was probably dead or interned, repeating her self-criticism or the stanzas in praise of Uncle Ho. He would never see her again.

In my dream a flower blooms... A sudden thought: Thu and the young girl in the tram... They resembled each other remarkably! He dressed in haste and went out, to the hospital. At the very least, he had to get news of the wounded girl.

Chapter 9

AT THE LUNG MUN, Johnny Kwok deliberately pushed customers and staff. And to be sure to annoy as many of them as possible, he went and sat at the back of the room, next to the toilets.

The waitress brought him his breakfast, a glass of soya milk and two fried pastry twists. He complained that the milk was not warm enough and the twists stale. A lie, but he got the satisfaction of seeing the girl change them for him.

"Bastards..." A powerful hint that the prices the little shit of a manager charged for his slop meant he could demand that it was edible.

After that he concentrated on the events of the previous day. He cursed these damned bombs, which exploded without warning and above all at the wrong time. Not surprising however, since they were built by these half-witted Reds. He had, nonetheless, probably made a mistake, for by neglecting this imponderable, his great plan had turned into a disaster.

And yet he had been watching them closely, these silly school kids who had started to mingle with the infamous lot at the Transport Union. Ah! This Siu Fung, alias Hung Kei, this Yeung Tak and the other braggarts who boasted about importing revolutionary upheaval into Hong Kong didn't suspect, when they went to the subversive meetings of the transport workers, that he followed closely on their heels and ignored not their slightest move, nor this ridiculous plot aimed at preventing the restoration of the transport.

A cowardly plan: these infantile idiots – who looked too naive to attract attention, or so their mentors certainly gambled – were to convey their bombs all the way to the depots that the unionists wanted blowing up. These slow-witted kids were hoping to practice on the trams before tackling the rest of the network. He, Johnny Kwok had, himself, discovered this pathetic project, and on his own would have caused it to fail by putting them all behind bars, Siu Fung and Yeung Tak on the one hand, their stinking commanders on the other, the moment the bombs arrived in front of the Percival Street depot in Causeway Bay.

But no, since these damned bombs... because of them, it is with him that his superiors picked a quarrel. They didn't appreciate that he had played it solo. But had he warned them, his plan would have been leaked within the hour, the hierarchy was so full of holes. He was criticized above all for having shot and killed this Yeung Tak. Well, it proved at least that he aimed accurately. And so what... did they or did they not want to crush these insurgents?

His superiors talked of suspending him. He didn't care. His present objective was to put the girl, Siu Fung, in jail. She had slipped through his fingers,

been thrown into space by the explosion. He had
hunted for her all night, banging on her parents'
door; peasants out of whom he had got nothing but
loathsome whining, and went through Wan Chai
with a fine-toothed comb. In vain. A real mystery,
but just wait and see, you bitch!

Chapter 10

SHE STAGGERED. EVERY step made her dizzy, like tottering on the edge of a ravine. There was certainly no danger, in the middle of this noisy bazaar which was Cross Street at shopping time. Forty pairs of arms per square metre would have stopped her from falling anywhere perilous. At worst she would have landed in a crate of mangoes, a box of octopus, a tray of raw meat, a mountain of underwear or a sea of shoes.

Yeung Tak... No, he couldn't have perished. He must just have been wounded, like her. She had to know. From a telephone box she rang his home. A woman, not his mother, answered. She asked to speak to her friend. Incomprehension at the other end of the line.

"Yeung Tak... for god's sake! Don't you know him?"

"No."

She hung up, not sure she had heard right. Was it due to the tumult of the crowd around her? The crowd and the smells, she normally didn't mind; today, their peculiar cocktail of freshness and mustiness, seasoned with a constantly changing zest of the undefinable, made her feel sick.

Bang! And yuk! Speaking of feeling sick… carried along by the human flow, she had just blundered into a bunch of goats' heads, freshly slaughtered, hanging outside a butcher's shop. A speciality of the district, which fortunately they didn't eat at home. These heads frightened her with their eyes rolled upwards, mutely crying the pain of their last moments.

"Shall I prepare one for you?" roared a jovial fellow with wrestler's forearms. With the point of his knife, he pricked the tongue of one of these bleeding trophies, as if to say: this is the best one. The butcher? Problem: she didn't remember him. The one who used to serve was skinny and old, and always with a dirty cigarette butt between his lips. Could this colossus be his son?

She chose to dash away without enquiring further. The thing was, suddenly, she realized that it was not only the butcher who was wrong. How many familiar faces among the shopkeepers? And even in the whole meandering crowd? None! Usually, she met at least two or three neighbours, to say nothing of the district's one or two famous skinflints, who could invariably be found at a specific time in a specific place, bargaining for a bunch of spinach or a pound of shrimps. "Hey it's becoming more and more expensive in your shop Mrs Tsang. Tomorrow I'll go somewhere else."

Just as bizarre, it seemed that men were wearing longer hair and ladies more colourful clothes with a different cut. These skirts so high above the knee, she had never seen anything like that! One could not

say that it was ugly, on those who had pretty legs...
but a bit decadent, wasn't it? With a brief look she
checked where her own dress ended, the one she had
taken from the girl in the next hospital bed. No, this
one, with large pastel flowers and too big for her,
remained decent. Besides, with the dressings on her
calves, she was not going to excite a lot of males.

The street signs also troubled her. She counted
many more than usual... Two, three times as many!
The same with the buildings. Behind the old houses
of Cross Street, they had multiplied like bamboo
during the rainy season; and they had become so
high and narrow that she wondered how they could
stand, unless they were defying the laws of physics...

Truly, she was hallucinating! Like some nights
when she was really tired, in between sleep and
consciousness, feelings of vertigo swept over her –
an immensely sheer cliff, an unending plain
stretching into the horizon – which she could only
get rid of by pinching herself. She did that now, to
recover her normal vision. But the buildings
remained huge. Had she been wandering through the
hall of distorting mirrors at Lai Chi Kok Amusement
Park she wouldn't have seen them differently. But
she was neither in Lai Chi Kok, nor in her bed. The
weakness of her convalescence was not solely to
blame. Something else was confusing her senses. But
what?

"Aren't I silly!"

The drip. They had drugged her at the hospital.
Logical, obvious! Those conspiring doctors had
wanted to turn her into a vegetable before passing

her onto the authorities. And now that she thought about it, the stranger with the hairy hand wasn't he a cop, an English big shot, a chief? "Fix her up, this suspect, so we can question her!" Definitely, she did well in slipping away.

Her parents lived close by, but the police were probably watching their flat. Anyway, at this moment she didn't feel like seeing them. Above all, she had to walk, had to sweat, had to eliminate the poison from her body.

Johnston Road, the cars all lined up, polluting the air with their smelly exhausts. The daily traffic jam, except that... all these vehicles, hadn't they got longer or were they smaller, rounder or more angular – she was very confused – hadn't they been subjected to a strange metamorphosis, just like everything else? Four or five trams arrived, in a bunch. Failure of the strike? Regrettable, but the ABC of any insurrectional strategy taught that Anti-Revolutionaries proved capable of mobilizing last minute forces out of despair, whenever they realized they were close to defeat. These short-lived bursts were not worth worrying about.

"What the...!" she hissed.

It was incredible, pinch me, slap me, bite me to chase this new illusion out of my brain. On a poster covering the whole side of the first tram, a brazen young girl was lazing around on a flying sofa, listening, blissfully, to music in earphones linked to a small box. 'Walkman, music in motion' proclaimed this phantasmagoria. Exactly as she had imagined during her tram ride.

No more doubt remained: she had been administered strange substances at the hospital, not in small doses and probably of different types. Such toxic combinations proved to be most dangerous, she had recently read in the *Young Pioneers' Magazine*.

Eat. Eat and gain strength: she needed that too, to fight against the poisoning. The smell of the cakes coming out of the oven of the Happy Cake bakery was pleasing to her nostrils. Dilemma... Mrs Leung, the shopkeeper, a friend of her mother's and a first class gossip, would tell the whole area about her visit. Siu Fung, carefully, walked past the shop. Another surprise, it was not Mrs Leung behind the counter, but a young employee whom she didn't know. She went in.

"A red bean bun, please."

"One dollar sixty."

"But..."

"What?"

"No, nothing."

She was not in a position to argue. All the same... when was the last time she had bought a red bean bun? Let's say, three or four days before. The baker had put up her prices tremendously, yet she wouldn't normally have thought of her as a speculator or profiteer. Hmm...

Coming out of Happy Cake, she noticed a red and yellow sign opposite. The 'Wellcome' the nurses had been talking about! Indeed a shop, and huge at that. Curious she had never noticed it before.

She crossed the street and pressed her nose against the window. A new phenomenon: smart housewives pushing steel trolleys among fully stocked shelves, even over stocked... a good sign, this: so much food, it could only be the work of Communism. Wellcome must be a symbol of the Party, like China Products, which she noticed nearby. Cleared away, all traces of the police violence! Redecorated, rebuilt and reopened, the shop must be full of wonderful things. Nothing, ever, would stop the march of the Great Revolution.

With happiness in her heart, she pushed on to Wan Chai Road. The Cathay cinema was showing a Kung-Fu film 'Something or other from Shaolin' with Jet Li, some runt actor, an unknown in her collection of stars. All these gaps in her memory were becoming annoying. When would the effect of this damned drug wear off? Not soon unfortunately. A newspaper vendor passed her, haranguing the passers-by with the latest issue of *Ming Pao*. The headline: 'One Country, Two Systems' almost made her faint.

Chapter 11

"SHE'S NOT HERE!"

The nurse seemed to blame Chambon. Wasn't she right to be angry? The kid had gone too far: "Yes sir, I'm certain. The clothes and the money of the patient who shared her room!"

He felt he had to ask how much "the little thief" had "borrowed". The nurse spared him no details, before handing him, in exchange for his "compensation for damages", the "young lady's belongings".

"They're all yours..."

To show that it was not the policy of a respectable hospital to hold on to the clothes of an offender.

Slightly confused, Roger abandoned the idea of going straight home. He found himself, without knowing why or how, *en route* to the Sikh temple. Idiot: this puffed-up meringue-like structure most of the time brought to mind adjectives for which 'nauseous' was a polite alternative. You'd better go and get your hair cut... He turned back, heading for his hairdresser.

His hairdresser, his street, his district... As if he were a local, he a native of Rochefort-sur-Loire. But it was true, he did say my hairdresser, my street, my district when he talked about them, because he had felt at home, comfortable, for the ten years he had been living here.

Arriving in Hong Kong, one year before the 'liberation' of Saigon by the Comrades, he had first stayed in a hotel: the Asia lodge in Causeway Bay. He walked around the area during the weekends. That was how he had come across Stone Nullah Lane, in Wan Chai. Strange name and multicoloured houses – green, yellow, blue – this narrow street, at the foot of the hills up to the smart residences of the Mid-Levels, led onto a temple, clouded in incense, dedicated to Pak Tai, the god of the North. 'Flat for Rent', he read on the door of a building facing this sacred spot. He went in. Despite its state of disrepair, the place drew him. Its balcony offered a view onto an area which reminded him very much of Saigon's back streets, where one could find everything one needed: the grocer, the dry cleaner, the electrician, the shoe repairer, the noodle restaurants.

What's more, the area provided an unexpected industry: garages. One counted no fewer than five or six around his block. These dens, black with grease, dealt only with the cream: Jaguar, Mercedes, Aston Martin or Porsche, god knows why, in this miserable hole! Roger had never driven anything other than his father's old van, before the army. The perfectly designed bodies, the shiny chrome, the gear boxes as precise as chronometers, the mahogany dashboards and the full grain leather upholstery, fascinated him.

The following Saturday, he moved into Stone Nullah Lane. He was still living there. Although the developers of the towers that were being built around him tried to woo him, "You will have all modern comforts", he was not planning to move out. "Your skyscrapers don't amuse me… on the ground floor you can't see anything, and at the top, you get vertigo."

At the hairdresser's, he installed himself in the only armchair and started to read the *South China Morning Post*. The barber, who was drinking tea in the back room, came close knowingly. The French man had already been the week before. He didn't really need a haircut, more a moment of calm, which the man was proud to provide. A few clips just to make sure, a good massage and as many hot towels as he wanted… He silently started the execution of these custom made services.

'One Country Two Systems' left Chambon impassive. The agreement would not be signed for a while, the British would resist it and a lot of water would flow under the bridge before its implementation. In short, a new move was not yet on the cards and anyway would not be his concern: SCOMDEF would retire him well before that.

On the 'news in brief' page, he looked in vain for the story of an explosion or a fire, which would have explained his encounter during the night. Perhaps this kind of incident was too common in Hong Kong to be reported.

Down at his feet, the red plastic bag containing the young girl's clothes was rapidly being covered with fine grey hairs from the hairdresser's clipper. Tiny snow flakes… He thought that by going round the schools in the neighbourhood, he would eventually trace the runaway. Yes but what for, aren't you busy enough as it is with your Taiwanese?

Back at home, he pulled a file out of his desk drawer and stapled Kuang's business card to it. Then he called Lavinier to talk about the case. The military attaché didn't answer. Never there when he is needed this one, duly noted, he would manage without this slacker. He inserted a sheet in his typewriter. The beginning, still unclear, of a preliminary report to Paul Germain: the name and profession of his contact, his needs, the products likely to meet them, the financial conditions and eventual means of payment. Not easy. Vigorous confidentiality, imperative for this market, complicated arrangements: shell companies, middlemen and commissions – inevitably.

"Pain in the arse!"

He had neither motivation nor concentration. The girl's clothes bothered him still. How many schools to visit, if he set about doing that? He grabbed the telephone directory: colleges and secondary schools, Wan Chai… Rosary Hill, Queen's, Marymount, Saint-Paul's, etc. He counted about ten in this neighbourhood. The task of one morning, if he organized it well.

Why not tomorrow? Pleased with this plan, he returned to his IBM.

Chapter 12

EVOLUTION IS NOT a dinner party. But how about what was happening to her? She shut herself in the public toilets. Dirty, her hair greasy – at least the bits that the explosion had not burnt – her own image in the mirror, with its vacant stare, lost, extremely weary, frightened her. She washed her face, banging her forehead against the mirror, so hard that it cracked, but she was still there, aching and bloated, a wild apparition of her real self.

She wandered around Wan Chai, far too bewildered to go elsewhere, and spent the night in the garden of the Pak Tai temple. To think, she had always wanted to sleep outside! But although the sky was as starry as the dome of her school's chapel, it was also heavy with battalions of mosquitos and filled with weird and worrying noises. The wooden bench she occupied seemed to have been designed for torture. Not much sleep…

Two salty duck eggs and a glass of tea in a small outdoor restaurant in Stone Nullah Lane. Her breakfast over, she found herself nodding off. To sleep, really.

Why not at the Cinema Cathay, when it opened? Fashion Week, the latest autofocus Polaroid…

stunning adverts that kept her awake. On the other hand, the kung fu film was unexciting. She quickly dropped off, just after the Master had graduated his latest class of disciples, among whom was a funny one who, when she woke up, had betrayed that good man twenty six times. Regrettable behaviour although predictable: the face of this professional Judas in the opening scene would have dissuaded any short sighted mole from betting a *kuai* on his honesty, so the venerable Master, a hundred and sixty years old next summer but with the wisdom of a ten year old initiate, didn't quite deserve his title, giving his trust to such a lout. As for the previously mentioned Jet Li, the honest and faithful follower and righter of wrongs, he didn't exactly sparkle. Daft, these modern films!

The day was ending when she came out. At Yeung Tak's, it was probably time to eat. A good moment to try her luck again.

"Hello?"

A male voice this time, but still unknown to her.

"Yeung Tak?"

"Who?"

"Yeung Tak, someone who lived in the building… He may have moved?"

"Hmm, hold on."

A crackling, the man talking to people in the room, other voices answering.

"Yeung Tak, the boy killed by the police, at the time of the riots?"

Cold tears came down her cheeks as the receiver slipped out of her hand, to swing, squawking a long chain of tinny "hellos" like a hanged parrot, before falling silent.

She walked away. Who, and what to turn to now? The stranger on the tram? Contrary to what she had previously thought, she didn't see him as a policeman anymore. She wished she had checked whether he had left his name at the hospital. Did he live in the neighbourhood? Even if he did… What more could he do for her? Her case was unimaginable, hopeless.

Her parents, then? She didn't feel up to going to Lee Tung Street… but she couldn't possibly stay where she was, walking up and down and feeling sorry for herself! She went back to the telephone and dialled the number of the tram company. Her father usually worked late. Someone said, no, sorry, they didn't know who she meant.

"A mechanic… Well, he was before…"

"Before what?"

Before what, indeed? Memories of Sundays. For a whole period, around the age of seven or eight, her father used to work on Sundays and she and her mother would join him at lunch time, at the Causeway Bay depot. They used to bring lunch to eat with other families, in the canteen. Then she would climb on board tram 120, the oldest of the fleet. All in wood, the driver's cab had metallic handles polished to a fine sheen through years of use. She pretended to drive, said that she was going to the sea, that the 120 was turning into a boat, that she was crossing the ocean… One day, a section head, a new one, came by: "This is not a playground, and as for your picnics in the canteen…"

The following Sunday, her father came home to eat and they never went back to the depot. Wasn't it also because of this humiliation that she had wanted to blow up the tram?

It was dark now. She had her hair cut on the pavement, very short, like a boy, and bought herself some men's clothes from a second-hand shop. She changed at the back of the shop. In this disguise, she decided to go to Lee Tung Street.

People also called it Street of the Printers, who were located there in large numbers. Their noisy machines beat out a heavy rhythm which possessed you as soon as you entered the street. All gone, all over. The printers had vanished, and the place was given over to a general hubbub emitted by who or whatever had replaced them, a bird shop, a mahjong shop, a Filipino grocer's shop, a hardware shop, themselves living on borrowed time: so many houses where no one lived anymore, with sealed doors and windows. Some large panels riveted onto their facades announced the imminent construction of needle towers even higher than those which had gone up all around.

At number 23, already demolished, stood a crane and a fence. The place would soon be called 'Noble Garden'. Thirty-two storeys, one hundred and twenty-five flats from studios to five-rooms, air-conditioning everywhere including the lifts, spectacular view, fire equipment, twenty-four hour security guards, as well as everything necessary for residents to enjoy 'the refinement of a VIP life in an exceptional environment'. Siu Fung could not quite see the value of the project: where would they put their 'Garden', the builders of this ugly and pointed thing? And her father and her mother, where had they sent them?

"The dressmaker, at number 23?" she asked the bird shop owner who was taking in his cages and about to close. He stared at her as if she had just fallen out of the sky. Although she hated them, at least in a certain way, the idea that her parents could be dead was even more heartbreaking than the death of Yeung Tak... An orphan? Goodbye solitude, hello nothingness! But no, my dear, you're out of your mind! Knowing her parents – above all no scandal – they had probably accepted the first offer of rehousing, without arguing, far away in the New Territories, Fan Ling or Yuan Long. Hence the fact that her father was not employed on the trams anymore. She would enquire, later.

On Wan Chai Gap Road, above the old post office, other empty buildings were doomed for destruction. One of them drew her attention. It seemed to have been recently abandoned, but the operations of expropriation were not quite complete, for there was still a semblance of life: a letter box with mail inside, some washing drying at a window, and even a service entrance left open, at the back. She entered and walked up the dark stairs. On the top floor, she arrived at a flat which a street lamp bathed in a pallid light. She pushed the door open. A few unstable pieces of furniture lay there, in the dust: two stools, a table and a bed with a mattress which must have dated from the Qing Dynasty, but, well, it would still be better than the bench at the Pak Tai temple. She collapsed onto it.

The following day, she returned to the small restaurant on Stone Nullah. Her general situation was not that good. A *wonton* soup and that was it, she was left with no money. It was like the end of a sad film. Next to her, children were quarrelling over sweets, a seller was bellowing the praises of her *tofu fa* and some old people were playing chess on a door step. The glaring sunshine projected their shadows so clearly one could believe that they actually existed without their creators. Wasn't it rather she, ephemeral traveller from an unreal world, a little cloud fallen out of its sky, who could not exist?

Then she saw, glittering in a bright light, the large watch, Orient, she remembered it clearly, which two days before indicated half past midnight when she would have sworn it was hardly ten o'clock. Its owner, a foreigner – she had been right – was coming out of a house opposite the temple, his index finger forming a hook, holding a red plastic bag.

Tall, huge, his face square and craggy, his rigid gait and his austere clothes, he looked like a labourer or a soldier. Not young any more: in his sixties, and with that a missing hand, the right hand. In short, she was discovering that the person who had saved her life was an old, one-handed, *gweilo*. Not exactly the best cards to hold if she envisaged soliciting his help…

She remained fixed at the table of her cheap restaurant. Well! At least she now knew where he lived. Perhaps she would approach him, after all, when he came back.

Chapter 13

EANING COMFORTABLY AGAINST the low wall surrounding the garden of Pak Tai temple, Inspector Kwok was greedily picking from the carton of chicken feet that he had bought from a hawker on Hennessy. Bought? Well… the peasant had had no license. "No papers at all, a pure illegal" was what his look of unkempt mainland yokel trumpeted louder than a Tibetan horn. That was bad luck, or good luck, depending on your point of view, Johnny had got him to understand, when he mentioned that he was a cop…

The yokel would have given him half of his takings.

"What? You think I am a corrupt cop? I could take that badly, you idiot. Give me a helping and clear off; and I don't want to see you around here again!"

It was just a joke. Kwok was in a cheerful mood. Some days were like that, one could in all honesty be proud of oneself, and find everything was sweetness and light. His new friends from Beijing, for whom he was now working on the side, as his police job paid so badly, had 'commissioned' him to do a bit of cleaning up among the Taiwanese and their connections, in relation to the return of Hong Kong to the motherland. They were going to be happy, and would surely increase his 'salary'. But enough talk, it was time to act. Chambon, this French pig who thought he could steal the moon, had just come out of his front door. Johnny threw his empty carton into an incense bowl, and headed for the building.

*

Siu Fung did not at first pay much attention to the man whose silhouette, swollen, yet very ordinary looking, came from the temple and approached the entrance to the foreigner's house. But why was he peering furtively to the right then to the left, as if to make sure that nobody was looking?

These moves revealed his profile and she almost cried out in shock. The bloody cop from the tram! She would have recognized him among a hundred others, even in his coffin! He was not wearing his ridiculous fake moustache any more, but his now bloated features remained those of a wild beast, from which emanated an aura of depravity. How could he reappear at this instant, in this place?

He pulled something out of his pocket: a bunch of keys. Did he too live here? Unless… the foreigner was a policeman after all, to whom the bloody cop was coming to report? But you don't enter people's homes when they are not there. In fact he tried his keys one after the other until the right one opened the door.

And so? And so it was clear: Yeung Tak's killer

was continuing to investigate her. He had traced the old one-handed man who had rescued her, and he had come to search his place.

Siu Fung renewed her hate for him; a hate coming from deep within her, pouring feverishly out of all the pores of her skin. Simultaneously, there was instilled in her the desire to protect the foreigner from this evil monster.

*

Already five schools, where Chambon had been told that no, unfortunately, the uniform he was showing them was not one of theirs. At the sixth, Saint-Francis Canossian, the headmistress, a woman still young, wearing her hair in a bun and a discreet cross around her neck, welcomed him as if he were a parent, and he, who had never had children, stated his problem as if he wished to be... with respect and a slight anxiety in his voice.

"I see..."

Miss Wilson, that was her name, punctuated in this way each of his sentences to encourage Roger to continue, he who was already asking himself if all this was worth it. In the end he showed her the girl's torn blazer. She frowned.

"May I?"

The headmistress felt the material, examined the burns and looked with interest at the torn pocket on the blazer where the badge should have been.

"Where did you get this from, and when?" she asked, obviously puzzled.

He completed his explanation with the incident at the hospital, the running away of the young girl and his quest to find out who she could be. "In short, this intrigues me", he summed up.

And he added, to appear more rational, that he had lent money for the medical care that the family, if he found them, might well reimburse him.

Miss Wilson resumed running her hands over the material.

"You are certain of what you're telling me, I mean… the circumstances, the tram, the young girl?" she asked, in a strangely embarrassed tone.

Chambon answered yes, of course, he had not been dreaming.

"I see," she repeated. "I see…"

And he, less and less.

Chapter 14

IN NEED OF A PICK-ME-UP, and of verifying something, Roger sat looking at the collection of black and white newspaper photographs which covered one of the walls of his club. Framed in dark wood, they evoked bygone eras of Hong Kong. How many times had he looked at them, without seeing them? One in particular. It showed soldiers wearing caps and shorts and with guns, guarding a group of men crouching on the ground, their hands behind their heads. 'The 1967 Riots', the caption indicated.

"It's not possible. That woman must take me for a fool!" he mumbled before emptying his glass and leaving.

*

Siu Fung entered the temple garden and stood behind a big banyan tree, very close to the bench where she had spent the night.

The bloody cop left the foreigner's place after fifteen minutes, went to telephone from the grocer's shop then came into the temple garden and sat on the bench, so near that she could hear him breath. Another ten minutes. A police Toyota parked nearby.

The young cop who got out, looking very clean, came straight over and sat down next to him and handed him a newspaper, without a word.

Good news? The bastard read with interest and even delight the article that the clean cop pointed out to him.

"Well done Andy, good work", she heard him say.

Then nothing. The duo remained there, on the bench, saying nothing, stretching occasionally. No need to be a fortune teller to guess that they were waiting for the return of the foreigner. Siu Fung didn't dare move. She was finding the time crawling along slowly and the ants crawling up her legs, annoying. And then, phew, Andy stood up. But not phew! the bloody cop remained seated, his eyes following his partner, who ambled nonchalantly to the grocer's. He came back with two cans of soft drinks and some peanuts. They toasted each other. *Aya*! She was thirsty too! You pigs.

At last… The *gweilo* came home, still carrying his red plastic bag. He seemed pensive, uncertain. The two sleuths exchanged a crafty look but did not yet react. God, if you knew how much I feel like strangling you! They calmly finished their drinks and let him go inside the building before getting up and approaching it themselves.

Coming out of her hiding place, Siu Fung stretched her limbs and seized the newspaper that they had left.

'Taiwanese National Murdered'. The title of the article was underlined in red. About fifteen lines recounted the drama:

This morning, at around ten, the police discovered the body of a man floating in the harbour. He had been killed by a bullet in the head. Rapidly identified thanks to the papers he was carrying, Kuang Hsien-Bian was a senior executive of the National Centre of Strategic Studies of Taipei, an organization with a respectable image but which experts believe is a covert nationalist centre for the acquisition of military equipment. Kuang's passport showed evidence of no less than eight trips to Hong Kong during the past six months. What was he coming here to do, if not to negotiate contracts with arms dealers and foreign secret services many of whom, it should be remembered, hide behind respectable facades but behave in a very dubious manner in the colony? This illicit milieu is naturally disposed to violence. Kuang probably perished following such an undoubtedly sordid dispute. This horrendous crime sounds a wake up call to the British authorities, who should re-establish order in the territory over which they have temporary charge, in order to leave it perfectly safe for their Chinese counterparts who will legitimately retake possession of it in a few years, with the goal of turning it into a haven of peace and morality in the region.

Siu Fung instinctively said to herself, there are a lot of things I don't get in this load of rubbish, but something is clear: they are going to arrest the foreigner and accuse him of this murder.

Chapter 15

CHAMBON WAS ANNOYED when the door bell rang. No sooner was he back than he was being disturbed. The two weirdos on his landing, distorted through the spy-hole, didn't make him feel any better: the first one looked like a fat-jowled beaver force-fed with malevolence, the second one looked a little too much like a well-bred boy not to be something of a hoodlum.

"What do you want"? he asked from behind the door.

"Police, we would like to talk to you…"

He opened the door carefully, not without an unpleasant premonition: this is alfa bravo, serious frigging hassle at two o'clock…

"Inspector Johnny Kwok, my colleague Andy Tam."

Fat jowls, whose face on closer inspection looked not only like a beaver but also – ugh! what a disgusting mix – like a sewer rat, started on a long spittle-filled monologue of which Roger only took in the essentials: Kuang, his Taiwanese, had been killed, the body fished out of the harbour, and his own name card in the dead man's wallet.

As a result of which, these detectives would be

grateful if he could spare them a moment of his time, in order to answer a few questions.

"Just checking, routine…"

Frigging hassle? Rather an understatement, Roger. There was the sheet of his report, still inserted in his typewriter in evidence on his desk which, although not including details, furnished nevertheless some transparent information on the nature of the early relationship between the deceased and him. There was also his Manurhin revolver, hidden under a pile of clothes in his wardrobe, for which, in all truth, he did not have a license. If these super sleuths found it…

Had he any right to oppose them? Most probably, but he didn't exactly know which and moreover presumed that his visitors, outwardly polite but contemptuous deep inside, would not give a damn about his rights.

*

In the first garage, at the end of the street, Siu Fung pinched a screwdriver and a hammer. She went back to the Toyota and started to walk around it, all innocent-like. Suddenly:

Bang ! Pssshhh…! A heavy blow to the rubber, and a first tyre was punctured. Then a second, then the four of them, for good measure. Satisfied, Siu Fung dropped the tools where she stood and returned to the temple and its banyan tree.

The foreigner came out of the building, escorted by the two cops. No handcuffs, because of his stump probably, but obviously they were taking him in. They directed him into the back seat of their vehicle, where Kwok also installed himself. The young cop took the wheel. The engine rumbled. The punctured tyres slid badly on the tarmac. The driver persevered. Mistake: he bumped into the car in front and stalled.

"Fuck! What is this shit?" Kwok yelled.

People heard him from a long way away, because he had his window down. A jolly crowd formed, one of whom was the mechanic from next door, who seemed not a little surprised to find his tools in the gutter.

Siu Fung appeared, opening wide the car door.

"This way!"

The foreigner seemed to hesitate, to not understand, then decided to jump out of the car.

Chapter 16

THE OLD MAN had fled, of little importance. On the contrary even, he would catch him again and running away proved his guilt more than ten thousand pieces of evidence.

Siu Fung on the other hand… Where did she come from, like a little Jack in the Box, to land in Stone Nullah Lane and throw a spanner in the works by helping the French man? Huge and disturbing mystery. Her short hair and her ridiculous male outfit didn't change anything, she was radiant, as fresh, as desperately pretty as before!

He, Johnny Kwok, had got paunchy, flabby, bald… His soul, of course, that was something else. He felt more treacherous, more experienced in maliciousness, stronger, in a word! This reassured him. So the silly girl had thought fit to again cross his path? She would pay for it this time, definitely!

*

Chambon had not run like that since Indochina. Dripping with sweat, out of breath, he collapsed. The girl gave him some water that he drank as thirstily as he had done with the spring water from the Hong

Lien mountains, in the old days. Sweet agony, delicious breathlessness, resurrection… on a filthy mattress with springs like undernourished kid's navels. He scanned the dirty room.

"Where are we ?"

"Wan Chai Gap Road."

They had run in all directions to come back, almost, to their starting point, Siu Fung explained rather proud of herself, as if she had just invented the thirty-seventh stratagem. Didn't the fact that the foreigner himself had not noticed, demonstrate her instinct for navigation?

"Did you recognize me?" she asked, more serious now.

Nodding positively, he muttered: "The tram, the hospital." He would have liked to tell her: "I tried to find you when you left, I am happy to see you again and thank you for rescuing me from the clutches of the police". Although, objectively, her initiative had put him in an even deeper mess, it was the thought that counted. He would have liked to add: "Tell me a little bit more about yourself and what really happened to you on the night of the tram". But nothing came out of his mouth. All the same, she seemed to read his thoughts and, with a gesture, indicated that they would talk about it later.

"I bet that bloody cop is accusing you of having bumped off the Taiwanese!"

He was flabbergasted. First, the expression 'that bloody cop', as if she knew him personally. And above all, how could she have heard about Kuang? Realizing that the foreigner was floundering, Siu

Fung gave him the newspaper folded inside her outfit.

"The policemen left it on the bench where they were watching out for you, down at the temple. The whole story is there."

"The story, which story?"

"About the Taiwanese, of course!"

She summed up the article for him, and finished with a questioning pout.

"You are right, they want to make people believe that I am the assassin", he sighed while massaging his eyebrows.

He didn't want to say more. In the state he was in, it would have complicated everything. The very fact of explaining the cop's conspiracy, crude as it was, was difficult: the one named Kwok had straight away asked him if he possessed a gun and which make it was. He hadn't allowed Chambon time to reply, had gone straight to his wardrobe, lifted up the right pile of clothes, had seized the gun, and thrown it to him. Chambon had caught it in mid-air, putting his finger prints all over it, only to realize that it was not his Manurhin, but a Czech gun, no doubt exchanged for his while he was out. Without even trying to hide his hands, which Roger had then noticed were gloved, Kwok had proclaimed, "What a coincidence, it was exactly a toy of this calibre which had been used to send Kuang to meet his maker."

"Are you really what the newspaper says, an arms dealer or a secret agent?"

Sharp girl, eh! All right, he could not avoid a minimum of explanation. He let out without quibbling that yes, an arms dealer as you say; also that OK, he and the Taiwanese were in business, but he had not killed him, honest to God. Men, he had killed a few during the war. "When I caught it too, look at my empty sleeve". But this Kuang, no, to do away with him, what foolishness!

"Would you assassinate your clients?"

"Pff…"

"My name is Roger", he admitted. "I am French. And you?"

"Siu Fung. Well… People also called me Hung Kei, before. But now it's Siu Fung."

Before. Now. Often his words too. Funny. Peculiar. No, Roger, forget this nonsense!

"I too loath this bloody cop."

"So what did he do to you?"

"He killed my friend. Let's kill him and get out of here!"

Charming.

Chapter 17

JOHNNY KWOK LIKED to search through the archives alone. There he found peace and quiet, a bit like in a cemetery, except during the Ching Ming festival of course, this unbearable procession of noisy visitors to all the burial sites of Hong Kong and China. How come the dead had not yet found a way of shutting up these pests, considering how long this nuisance had gone on? But the archives, they offered the advantage of not having a Ching Ming: one did not have to fight through crowds in the department wanting to go down and sniff their mouldy smells, or be confronted by the tormented spirits; victims and killers, who lived there.

He immersed himself in them as pleasurably as others would in the hot springs of Conghua. The examples of universal depravity housed in this basement of the police station were endowed with an undeniable quality of consolation. And though some perverts might be upset by the idea, for the rest of us, one could always find worse than oneself there. Better than a quest for an unattainable virtue, this banal observation helped one to live. Johnny was surprised that so few people recognized it.

He dug out Siu Fung's file from his shelves, took it up to his office, but didn't open it. What was the point? He could have recited it by heart; *from* his heart. The memory of this whole affair tore at it with red hot tongs. It had cost him a reprimand and almost ten years without promotion, but that was a bagatelle: that's life, as one says. He had gambled, and lost. He had only himself to blame. Nothing to be angry about.

Siu Fung… He had loved her from the moment he first saw her, at the Transport Union, the little bitch. So pretty with her mother of pearl lips, her eyes radiating love… for that stupid Yeung Tak, the student leader who probably still wet his bed, this slug, this empty headed fool he would have liked to impale or split in two with an axe, this puppet he would happily have suffocated in a pit of manure, he would have gouged out his eyes, cut out his tongue, and grilled his balls on a barbecue… He had only killed him, with a bullet in his chest. A disappointment.

Siu Fung, who wanted people to call her Hung Kei, the Red flag! Idiot! Little Phoenix suited her so well. You must never disown your parents nor what they gave you, even if sometimes you can't stand them.

The father had kicked the bucket following a heart attack a few months after the drama. A trivial event, but the mother had dared to complain and came out with the allegation that on the night of her daughter's disappearance, Kwok came round to their house to interrogate them and had slapped her husband several times. He had never recovered from this and there was no need to look further for the origin of his heart attack. The old bat had even produced some doctor's certificate in support of her crazy accusations! Fortunately the judges had obfuscated the issue, and the mad woman had in the end cleared off, God knows where. He could certainly get his hands on her, by consulting a few files, and send her his best regards. But what was the use? She was probably not even aware that her child had just re-entered that great chorus of life we call the modern world.

Hung Kei, the Red Flag… even with such a formidable nickname, he would have adored her. She never saw a thing at the time, when he had followed them, her and the other smart arses. A proof of his professionalism. He almost regretted it. Had he approached her, wouldn't he have been able to convince her to leave those silly school kids and unionists? They might have married. No, Johnny Kwok and marriage do not go together, but… they would at least have been lovers.

And here she was reappearing, radiant looking, even younger than before. Yes, younger! And now, he was sure, it was not his love which saw this but his eyes, wide open and with unclouded vision – his eyesight had always been excellent, close up or at a distance. Siu Fung's youth was authentic, true, miraculous! First he certainly thought it was a pity that she had taken up with the French man. But wasn't it possible to regard this distasteful mismatch as a bit of help from fate? Hadn't Siu Fung teamed up with the arms dealer in order to find him, Johnny Kwok? Thank you Buddha, thank you Sky and all the spirits of the Earth, for the way the world had turned out.

"Right, back to work!"

It was not enough that the gods put Siu Fung on his path again. Now he had to make sure that she would not escape him again. Quick! An idea, a way to hold her, and eliminate Chambon for good. He had pulled such a face, the bum, when he discovered the Czech piece instead of his Manurhin! Listen, your Manurhin I threw it into the sea, and believe me, you will be joining it soon!

Chapter 18

"MAO TSE-TUNG ?"

"Dead."

"And Chou En-Lai?"

"Dead too."

"Who is in charge then in China?"

"Teng Hsiao-P'ing."

"That old scrooge? And in Hong Kong? 'One Country Two Systems', what does that mean?"

"Do you know at least which era we are living in?" scoffed Roger, slightly nervous all the same.

She changed the subject: "These arms, apart from the Taiwanese, who do you sell them to?"

"Most countries."

"Including China?"

"The occasion has not yet arisen, it would be a bit difficult at the moment, but who knows, maybe one day…"

"And your war, who was it against?"

"Vietnam…"

He didn't say communists. Nevertheless she burst out, half serious, half amused:

"You're nothing but an imperialist and a colonialist!"

They closed this chapter there.

Later, he asked some questions, without much success: her parents? Dead for a long time. Who was looking after her then? A flutter of her eyelashes meaning everything and nothing, that she was managing perfectly well by herself and that it was none of his business anyway.

Her friends, apart from the one that inspector Kwok had killed? None. And this sad story, when did it happen, and how?

"Too complicated to explain."

"Any connection with the tram?" he persevered.

"Yes, no, I mean…"

Yes, no, I mean… Call me an old woman if you like but don't teach your grandmother to suck eggs: I believe the answer is yes. Otherwise, you wouldn't have escaped from the hospital in case the cops, who were after you, picked you up. He thought all this but didn't say it, perhaps because of what the headmistress of Saint-Francis had told him.

"How did you find me?" he asked instead, paternally.

"By chance, in your street, a little before the cops came to arrest you. I had spotted them too, at the entrance to your building. I suspected they meant you some harm."

"And you wanted to come to my rescue?"

She nodded and he, very moved, got some things off his chest.

"You know, I looked for you after your 'escape' from the hospital. They gave me your uniform. I wanted to return it to you. I went to your college, I talked to the headmistress, a lady, quite young. She told me her name but I've forgotten it (a lie, he recalled it very well). You remember it, don't you?"

A rather artificial yawn as an answer.

"Anyway, your uniform… Apparently it's a design they don't make anymore. At least, according to her."

"What else did she tell you?"

"Well, some rather surprising things, about the past. I don't know much myself. I arrived later in Hong Kong. And you, Hong Kong history, does it interest you?"

A long silence, then: "The bombs. You sell them, but do you also know how to make them?"

Chambon couldn't find a reply.

Chapter 19

FOUR DAYS they have been hidden away in their hole. Roger escapes at dawn each day, through the building's back door, which leads to a narrow passage stinking of urine. Hugging the wall, he reaches the public toilets adjoining the indoor Wan Chai Market. That's where he washes, quickly. Siu Fung prefers to do this in the evening.

From a telephone box close by, he first called Lavinier, who urged him not to do so again.

"Should there be a snag, the contracting party will bear the consequences alone." Despair. The contracting party is not him, but SCOMDEF. So he tried to contact Paul Germain. It cost him a small fortune every time, for the switchboard operator made him hold the line, before answering inevitably that the boss was not available, in a meeting.

"Meeting, *mon cul!*" he said, last time, to the woman.

He doesn't phone anymore. He has one thousand, six hundred and twenty dollars left in his wallet. Enough to last one more week, but the *Ville de Marseille* had better not be delayed. The *Ville de Marseille*, of the Messageries Maritimes shipping line, is his ace in the hole; his 'get out of jail free' card.

The freighter, which calls at Hong Kong every other month, is due any day. Trinquet, its captain, a former seaman in the French Navy, is an old mate of his. In Indochina they had some good times together. He'll go and see him, and he'll get on board secretly and leave Hong Kong. The girl? He doesn't know. He hasn't mentioned this plan to her. In any case, he is not sure that Trinquet would take her.

She is the one who does their shopping. She goes to Wellcome, because one can help oneself, without talking to the shop assistants.

"You take, you pay, that's all", she explained to Roger.

He said he knew.

He also gave her something to buy herself some decent clothes. She chose a pleated skirt and a white T-shirt printed with a kind of strawberry garland. Now, she looks nice and modern.

"You are prettier like this."

He was even impatient to see her hair grow: "This haircut of yours, honestly, if you ask me…?"

It is evident that she doesn't want to.

Chapter 20

FOR FOUR DAYS Johnny Kwok has been nosing around, scouring and questioning. He is convinced that the old duffer and Siu Fung are hiding not far away. How could they have left Hong Kong?

The French man has not visited his bank, drawn out money, nor gone back to his place (where Andy keeps a permanent watch) to pick up some cash: there were five grand behind his fridge. They had confiscated these, to cover their overtime. He does not appear on the passenger lists of planes or ships, for either of the past few days or the coming few. Finally, his fellow countrymen in the diplomatic corps, whom Johnny keeps tabs on as well, do not show any desire of putting themselves at risk for him. The military attaché least of all: this coward keeps such a low profile that he even avoids nodding to the guard at the entrance to the consulate.

Anyway, Chambon has his back against the wall and it is not Siu Fung who will be able to pull him out of trouble. No matter how long it takes him, he doesn't need to worry, it is so obvious; these two will sooner or later get caught in his net. Even if just through weariness…

In fact, that morning, he had had a tip-off. He was back in the neighbourhood, searching for those seemingly insignificant details which sometimes reveal a different angle and throw a light into the darkness of an investigation. A man discreetly invited him along the shady path which goes up towards Kennedy Road, behind Stone Nullah Lane. He was the kind who perspired cowardice, despicable self-interest and dirty tricks. Johnny just can't stand these little shits. Nevertheless he followed him.

"Is there a reward, for whoever you're looking for?"

Johnny threw him a "shut up"! but only inwardly, while outwardly promising him something, we'll decide what later, as long as he was not being taken for a ride.

"Wan Chai Gap Road, number 4. They're there", the informer whispered from the corner of his mouth.

"How do you know?"

"I saw the *gweilo* near the market, two days ago. I followed him. Finally he entered the place I've just told you about."

He will go and see, tonight, with Andy.

*

"The bomb… it's for your bloody cop?"

"Yes. We kill him and we take off, I've told you. I don't want to stay here. And you, you're coming with me."

Leaving, thanks to a bomb. He wanted to laugh.

She was certainly right on one point though: he had to take off *vite*. His solution however, the *Ville de Marseille*, was more reasonable. And more realistic… She hadn't given any details about her own solution, sensing no doubt that he would think she was crazy. Wouldn't there be good reason?

Chapter 21

THE HEADMISTRESS OF HER COLLEGE, young? That was hilarious! The one who reigned in her day, Mother Richardson, a bad tempered old woman with a moustache, would have sent Roger packing, she hated men so much. What did this new headmistress actually tell him, apart from the fact that her uniform dated back twenty years, and so what?

"Oh God!" she suddenly became alarmed. The newspapers were bound to have mentioned a case like hers, quoting her name and Yeung Tak's. They may have kept the articles, at Saint-Francis. Would they have shown them to Roger?

No. He would have been more direct: "What's this all about, Siu Fung?"

But he had only insinuated things… He was subtle, was Roger, under his outer shell of clumsiness. However, he had not been able to figure out the whole truth, just glossed over parts, if that. The best thing was to keep playing the fickle female, and not to give up about the bomb, you give it to me or I don't like you anymore. He would give in, this former exterminator of communists who would not hurt a fly, this dealer in death who would be better off selling toys. She would find a way to transform him – which is all he wanted – into a grumpy but soft grandpa…

Might as well start straight away, now, while he was boiling some water for their evening meal, instant noodles, on a stove salvaged from the house's attic.

"The bomb?"

Chambon looked up. In the glow of the candle they used for lighting, Siu Fung appeared even more charming. But no, sorry, he couldn't play this game.

"So, how would *you* kill the cop?"

He wouldn't kill anybody. Was that clear? In a few days, he would take a boat and go back to France, or elsewhere, some place where nobody would come and pick a quarrel with him or get on his nerves with such extreme demands.

He stopped there. Stupid, he had let out his plan!

"Will you take me?"

They ate their noodles in silence, Siu Fung sulking and he meditating over his life which had evaporated as undeniably as the waters of ancient seas had turned into deserts. Later, when the candle went out, he took her hand and they fell asleep like this on their prickly bed.

Chapter 22

N MY DREAM a flower blooms… A carnivorous flower, a flower with a scent of powder? In the middle of the night Roger hears a creak, like the careful step of a hunter wanting to be totally silent but failing, because it's completely impossible.

Especially when the prey is a fox with an ear as keen as his who, in the jungle, when playing cat-and-mouse with the Viets, had learned to detect almost all the different noises of their approach: breathing, murmurs, clicks… The creak has become a sliding of padded feet, as if the intruders have decided to put on slippers. Chambon tries to pick out their image, to define the outlines of the threat. There are two of them, he would guess.

They are approaching the front door… They are there now. They grope for the lock, will soon realize that it's broken, and that anyone can come in; a veritable open house. A slight rustle, steel against cloth… They are drawing their guns.

He wakes Siu Fung, puts a finger to her mouth and orders her to make her way stealthily to the next room. Then he gets up, grabs a wooden plank and goes and stands flat against the wall, on the left hand side of the door.

"*Saint-Michel!*" he shouts all of a sudden, to trigger a burst in by his intruders.

As he expects, two men charge into the flat. With all his strength Roger hits the first one, who falls to the floor with a dull thud. The second, panicking, opens fire like a fool, wildly. Roger counts the shots: four, five, six… The clip is empty. He jumps on the shadow which writhes in the dark, knocks the man to the ground, kicks him in the jaw and for good luck hits him in the back with his plank.

He gets back to Siu Fung and they escape into the night, pursued by the cries of their neighbours and the lights that come on as they run along the street.

Chapter 23

ONE OF THE TWO COPS was dead, a fractured skull; the young cop, the one whose name was Andy Tam, the paper reported. His colleague, inspector Kwok, had also been badly injured but would recover. The article continued that they were on the point of arresting a French man, the main suspect in the murder of the Taiwanese. His name appeared in full in the article, marred by a spelling mistake: Roger Chamdon. In the following issue for sure, they would publish a photofit picture, or worse his photograph, for there were bound to be one or two lying around in his flat.

One killed and one seriously injured. What fury had come over him to attack the two men in this way? Did he think he was in a war? Had he wanted to show off in front of Siu Fung? See how well I protect you? Poor simpleton! Ah! She had really led him on with her posturing, her boyfriend killed by the cop, her bomb. A trap for horny rookies. He had jumped in with both feet.

God help him. Since last night, one could legitimately call him a murderer, and the police could, just as legitimately, try to get him. Understood, noted, but he was not going to go crying to his mother. Like cards, Roger. A new deal. Not very good, but it'll have to do.

They had found shelter in a disused warehouse in Tuen Mun. Almost a palace compared to Wan Chai Gap Road: two camp beds quite acceptable, some office chairs likewise, and even running water and electricity. Roger knew the place having done a little bit of business with the owner, Wong, a midget verging on the criminal who struggled to make a living with machine tools, but who also trafficked in arms in his spare time. SCOMDEF occasionally sold him one or two crates of automatics. The final client was probably a triad, and sometimes a little lubrication was necessary to release the cash, but never mind, all that was over now. Wong had recently taken his bits and pieces and settled in Shenzhen, the Chinese town opposite Hong Kong, which was starting to overshadow the colony.

"Of course, everything there is half as expensive as here!" he said to the girl.

"Ah!"

Well, let's not get sidetracked, they should have come to Tuen Mun in the first place, the cops wouldn't have flushed them out there, he thought, and I am a fool for not having thought of it before.

Chapter 24

JOHNNY, ON HIS hospital bed, wavered between pain and jubilation. The old French cretin had given him a real going over, but he was savouring in advance his revenge. In three or four days, he would be out. Out of the question to take the one week of sick leave which these irresponsible doctors had just prescribed for him. Chambon could not escape providing he didn't give him time to breathe. And since the old man had become fond of Siu Fung, he would start by taking care of her.

How old was she now? Let's see, sixteen at the time, plus… He had never been good at mental arithmetic. The age range he came up with did not match what he had expected, and the effort made him dizzy. He gave up. Everyone was older by the same number of years, that's all.

Every morning, Roger sent Siu Fung to buy the newspaper and do the shopping.

"Tomorrow, you go, I am fed up."

"Me? But I will be spotted…"

Perhaps so, but honestly what a pain the excursion was! She made a detour every time, never the same, so as not to be tailed. Extensive and bleak routes: the warehouse where they were hiding was not the only abandoned one. The entire zone presented only peeling walls and padlocked gates, with not a soul in sight, as if everybody had deserted to China. All this to end up in rows of shabby buildings, uglier than any she had ever seen. What's more, no Wellcome! Just a market where it was not easy to steal. Roger would have made a fuss if she had admitted it to him, but with the little money they had left, and the exorbitant price of things, they would have been close to starvation if she had had to pay for all their groceries. What kind of world did he live in, this guy, to have not the slightest idea about a budget for two!

When she got back to their refuge she would throw the paper at him and he would devour the maritime pages in order to find out about the movements of vessels. Frantic reading which always left him disappointed.

"What the hell is this ship doing?"

Depression for the rest of the day. Siu Fung even preferred to go out again and wander through the ghost factories, rather than put up with his brooding.

"Be careful at least."

One morning, at last: "The *Ville de Marseille*! That's it. She has arrived!"

Roger could have danced with joy. Siu Fung, on the other hand, remained impassive. Was it such good news?

They left Tuen Mun for the harbour. From the top of a hill overlooking the sea, shining under the sun, they saw the vessel berthed at the Modern Terminals.

"Magnificent, isn't she?" enthused Roger.

Tonight, he would go to the Mariners' Club, where Trinquet stayed when he put into port in Hong Kong.

Chapter 25

FIGUREHEADS IN THE LOBBY, leather armchairs, soft lampshades and engravings of old riggings on the walls… The Mariners' Club exuded an old-fashioned atmosphere of sanctuary.

British, Indian, American, Singaporean or German crews immersed themselves in the pregnant smells of ale, polish and tobacco, in conversations embroildered with the thread of a refined inebriation not tolerating any coarseness or raised voices.

These gentlemen of the sea honoured here the old and glorious maritime England, this great-great aunt with whom it is proper to be polite and respectful. They would unwind somewhere else, later in the night.

Minors were not admitted. Just as well, Roger did not want Siu Fung around. She had, despite everything, insisted on accompanying him to the door.

"I'll wait for you here."

Would he arrange a crossing for her too? He still hesitated. He would see how the conversation with Trinquet turned out.

As he approached the bar, he thought he could hear some French.

"You're from the Ville *de Marseille*?"

Two officers nodded.

"Is the captain here?"

They pointed to a table where a lean man was sitting alone, sipping at a whisky.

"But… it's not Trinquet?"

The men explained: Trinquet had had appendicitis out at sea. He disembarked in Aden. Boussu, the second officer had taken over command.

Damn! His venture had started badly. He didn't know anything about Boussu. How to approach him, present his request?

Roger went over to him, ill at ease. The new master of the *Ville de Marseille* didn't even offer him a seat. Roger, standing, laboriously declared his identity and his friendship with Trinquet. The other stared at him with a 'Yeah, yeah' kind of cynicism.

"What's it about?" he snapped eventually, frugal with his words and rather enjoying watching Roger get bogged down in his.

"I need a passage", Chambon started, although he had already understood that he might as well not have bothered.

"Illegal, I imagine", Boussu whispered with disdain. But before saying nay, added that if Trinquet was obliging, he was not: the security at sea, the reputation of the company, the good relationship with customs and immigration, etc., what would become of all that if we did this sort of thing for people in every port of call?

"Furthermore, I don't want to know the reasons of the persons concerned, note that I didn't ask for any explanation, but it's not usually too pretty, is it?"

Roger didn't persevere, nor did he listen to the end of the speech. He came out of the Mariners' Club and joined Siu Fung.

"So?"

"It's no."

"Never mind, we still have the bomb."

A vile egoist on the one hand, a crazy girl on the other. He was in a fine mess.

Chapter 26

BACK AT WORK. Johnny spent his morning in the office, sorting out his mail, skimming through the memos received while he was away and laboriously writing some himself. All this nonsense was good enough for his colleagues, all of them members of the Society of Office Clerks with Bad Backs! A waste of time, a mental torture. Had Chambon and Siu Fung actually managed to leave the territory? Impossible now to get this idea out of his head, that the two of them were having a good time, in France or elsewhere, she so delicate, so pure, he so decrepit, so disgusting. Sickening!

His administrative chores more or less fulfilled, he oiled his gun meticulously. This exercise relaxed him and he changed his mind; the runaways were still in Hong Kong. Even better, Siu Fung, far from being stupid, must have twigged what kind of degenerate pachyderm she was dragging along with her in the person of the French man. She had dropped him, it couldn't be otherwise.

And he, Johnny, would soon be putting holes in the rotting meat of the old baboon. The girl? Forgiveness? No, that was asking too much, but something subtle, sophisticated. Nothing fatal however, he didn't feel like killing her, but rather having her in his power until the end of her days, and his.

However he hadn't got a clue about where to start. Where were they holed up at present? Everything had to be started again from scratch, and at lunch time, at the Lung Mung, he got nervous again. He took it out on an obese cow who had had the audacity to invite herself to his table. She was taking up so much room that she was getting his back up.

"You think you are in your cowshed?"

*

Roger remembered the 'Bangalore torpedoes', those Vietnamese explosives cobbled together with some picric acid or anything that would blow up. A lot of fiddling about and some recycling, but they caused huge damage.

With his unit, he had, himself, placed some pretty nasty explosive traps in the jungle, to give the Comrades a taste of their own medicine, but for all that, he could not claim to be an expert. He had simply observed the blasters at work. Let's say he mastered the theory, if that. But that was not the problem, damn it!

He didn't want to kill the cop, full stop. One was enough, no need to overdo it and above all… above all Siu Fung was the problem. Siu Fung who had entered his life without asking his permission. Siu Fung and her absolutely unbelievable story. Siu Fung who wanted to push him into the abyss, who had started with her little hand in his, when he had pulled her aboard the tram. Why him? Ah! His existence would have been so much easier, if he hadn't seen her running along those tracks, as if fleeing from her earlier life. But no, I'm hallucinating here... I am hallucinating and I don't care about these irrational speculations: there is only one world, one past, one present and one future... Or is there?

"You have nothing better to do?"

She was getting on his nerves, scrutinizing him constantly, letting him stew in his own juices, pretending she could read him like a book. Did she think she was so smart? Well then, he was going to put her in her place.

"Your bombs, were they high-explosive or deflagrating?"

Her little face lit up with a huge smile. She got up and placed a gentle kiss on his forehead. Roger held back the big warm tear coming to his eye. "What the hell!"

Beaten hands down, Chambon. No resistance, a real wimp!

Chapter 27

KWOK WORKS AT the police headquarters in Admiralty. Arriving at around nine o'clock in the morning, he goes out at ten, to roam around Wan Chai. First he patrols Stone Nullah Lane. He goes up and down the street absorbing the atmosphere, a slow pace, a sneering face, nasty looks, the jaw moving in a strange circular way, as if he were re-educating it after the thrashing Roger gave him. Then he moves on to neighbouring streets, sometimes this one sometimes that, again and again. The residents nudge each other as he goes past. He hails anyone unfortunate enough to catch his eye, a school kid, a grandmother or a window cleaner, and bombards them with arcane questions which they are incapable of answering. He hurls abuse at these incompetents then looks elsewhere, going into stairwells when he sees open doors, and displaying his police ID aggressively in front of whoever dares to ask him what he is up to. In fact, he goes round in circles.

Siu Fung, on his heels, is becoming excited tailing him. Intuitive yet methodical, she likes to add spice to the game and sometimes spies on him from closer than one *zhang* without his realizing it.

He lunches early, at Lung Mun. His afternoons are more varied: a jewellery shop in Causeway Bay, a branch of the Jockey Club in Sheung Wan… other current investigations, which don't seem to captivate him quite as much.

Once, he went into a chic hotel on Queen's Road, and joined two men waiting for him on a sofa in the lobby. He seemed worried listening to them. Yet, at the end, she is certain, they slid an envelope into his pocket. Money, for sure!

That day, she abandoned him to follow these enigmatic benefactors. Hardly a hundred metres down the street they went into the premises of the Xinhua news agency, the eye of the Party in Hong Kong. Suspicious, very suspicious, but she did not want to go deeper into it.

Johnny returns to the police station at around five and calls it a day at six thirty, at the same time as most of his colleagues. A rather pitiful moment. Groups form, some go towards Wan Chai, others towards Central. They go for a drink. Kwok keeps out of things. No one invites him, they would in fact stop him joining in. He makes the first move and leaves, determined, his back straight, as if he still had somewhere to go.

In actual fact, he turns at the first corner and, once out of sight of his colleagues, he hangs around the area. He gets drunk on boredom, one might say. When he has had his fill, he hastens, everything else forgotten, towards the Lung Mun.

This is where he dines, alone, every evening: a meal quickly devoured. At eight, at the latest, he makes his way home to Quarry Bay – she followed him once all the way there.

And this idiot quite simply takes the tram.

Chapter 28

HE BOMB WAS a different kettle of fish. Between what they needed, ideally, and what they could get, easily, cheaply and without creating suspicion, there was a big difference.

"Must make a list", Roger pronounced knowledgeably the day he started to think about it seriously.

"Like for the shopping", approved Siu Fung.

Finding the parallel comical, she immediately brandished a piece of paper and a pencil, and waited for the dictation. Her attitude had the effect of annoying the French man: "I am not joking now."

It couldn't have been much fun being in the war with him every day.

"Sulphur, phosphorus, caustic soda, washing powder... Also get some strong glue and some electric wire. Go to several stores..."

Buying from only one would have risked giving the shopkeeper a clue as to the final use of the products. As a result, she spent two days gathering the ingredients, which were not cheap (a bulk purchase would have allowed them to obtain a discount).

They have almost no money left and this morning,

she stole three quarters of their food. Still saying nothing to Roger who, all the same, must have suspected something, because he was surprised by the prices she quoted. The cost of living in Tuen Mun would be, by her prices, roughly one quarter of that in Wan Chai. Also she stole some smart clothes. For them, when they leave. She has not shown them to him yet. He would complain too much!

However, despite his grumpy temperament, she is grateful to him. He has understood, otherwise he would not have accepted her plan. He understood without asking any of the questions that she dreaded as much as her own answers. He understood and he believed her, probably since his meeting with the headmistress of Saint-Francis and her story about the uniform which was no longer in use. All things considered, she is pleased to have him as a friend.

He perfected his mechanism, assembling and dismantling it a hundred times, and measuring, the same number of times, his mix of chemicals. Even so, he is not sure. He would like to conduct some tests, but where? They have only one chance, that's it.

"Are you ready?" Siu Fung asks him.

"Will have to be", he sighs.

She decided that they would act the following day.

Chapter 29

I T WILL START at the Lung Mun, in the evening, when Kwok comes out and stands at the tram stop to return to his place. Not very far from there, Siu Fung will show herself leaving the doorstep where she will have been hiding. The policeman will see her and set off in her pursuit. She will flee following the tram lines, right down the middle. She is fast, Kwok is slow and convalescent: he won't catch her up. She will run three or four hundred metres, all the way to the exact place where the bomb she had once been carrying had exploded, shortly after the junction of Johnston and Hennessy. Their strategy, otherwise, probably could not work. Roger will wait for them there.

He is wearing a beautiful blue and white striped shirt, clean and smelling new, that Siu Fung has pinched for him – yet another stupid thing – she is simply intractable! He doubts now that she ever resembled Thu, whose features, to be honest, he has practically forgotten, but who, in any case, was not a thief.

In less than a quarter of an hour, he is going to throw his device straight at the cop. A foolish act, childish, ridiculous, stupid and all the other synonyms he could find in the thesaurus, but he is going to do it.

He is going to do it for this little hawker of 'pineapples' – the term for the bombs at the time, the school headmistress told him – coming straight from 1967, the year of the riots in Hong Kong. It is of course a mirage, a tale, a coincidence, what else? But it doesn't matter. Like the Virgin Mary he had so many times wished he believed in…

He is going to do it for this insolent girl who has turned his dull autumn agenda upside down. He is going to do it because he doesn't want to dash the hopes she has put in him without ever telling him. This magic of the indescribable moves him more than anything else. Yes, he is going to help Siu Fung to recreate what she lived, or thinks she lived, seventeen years earlier in the tram. They are going to blow away Kwok, their common enemy, and vanish at the same time, just like that, off they go! No more Roger, no more Siu Fung. Why? Because she is all he's got left in the world and because he loves her.

Love? Dummy! Nothing in this whole sad story makes sense. He is standing there, as rigid as a pike, with his lousy device which he doesn't even know is going to work. In fact, Siu Fung is not even going to arrive, skipping along the tram lines, neither is the cop going to chase her. He has been dreaming from the beginning. She doesn't exist. Neither does Kwok. Or, they are two con artists who have made fun of him, have made up a sordid farce… How come he has swallowed this nonsense? He is going to wake up, gather his thoughts and at last discover the catch in all of this, the trigger that fired off all this madness. Tomorrow, he will return home and get back onto the treadmill. He will remake contact with the still-alive Taiwanese, finish his report for SCOMDEF and follow up on all his clients, the Malaysians first, going on for six months now, with their salamats for second-hand bazookas...

And even if the girl shows up, what will it prove? He is going to die along with the cop. As things stand, he'll make sure that, at the last minute, he moves Siu Fung out of the way, puts her out of reach. He has attached a piece of string to his bomb. If he can, he'll get near enough to Kwok to tie it around his neck. He will knock him to the ground if needed, and they will be blown up together. Is there really any alternative? There are still lots of people around. Being killed along with the cop, acting as a shield, that is all he can think of to avoid innocent deaths. Dying does not bother him. It should have happened ages ago, with his mates, on the Black River...

Bloody hell! Here comes Siu Fung! She is running fast and yet Kwok is following on her heels, staggering a bit but swifter than expected. Ten metres separate them... The blast is going to kill them both. Faster! he would love to shout, but it's too early for him to reveal himself.

*

Behind them a tram is coming, the driver is sounding the klaxon to make the two weirdos running in the middle of the track move away.

One final effort and Siu Fung will be level with him. She sees him, waves her hand, gasps, can't do anymore. The cop slows down, and even stops. Good God! He's going to pull out his gun and shoot Siu Fung like a dog. Acting immediately, Roger leaps out of his hiding place and charges.

"Lie down!" he orders the girl.

She lets herself fall, exhausted. Kwok goes rigid, disconcerted by the rush of the French man rendered red by the street's neon lights. But he reacts and opens his jacket. Double or quits! Roger realizes that the bugger has enough time to aim. So, he stops, his bomb secure in his hand. He excelled, in the past, in throwing grenades. With his thumb, he activates the detonator…

Kwok, startled again, lifts his eyes to the sky. What is this unidentified flying object gliding towards him? Chambon moves towards Siu Fung. He literally jumps on her, crushes her under his hundred kilos. He hears her sigh and blocks her ears, one second before the roar of the explosion and its devastating tongue of flame.

Chapter 30

OHNNY KWOK FELT HIMSELF irresistibly sucked into the flames, drawn *manu militari* into a furnace. He literally melted, distended, burst, to better disperse and merge with the surroundings which too were in considerable disarray. Like horses on a carousel, Chambon's mask of rage and Siu Fung's fragile and graceful features, forever young, one last time crossed his field of consciousness, then disappeared, like a dove in the hands of a magician. Strange impressions, followed by a heavy fall… He found himself on his back, in his socks, between the rails. The ringing of a bell pierced his ears, together with a horrible screeching sound. He turned his head. 'Ipad 2, thinner, lighter, faster', he read underneath the photograph of the flat object, smooth and completely unknown which adorned the nose of the tram bearing down on him.

The vehicle passed over his body, separating him, almost painlessly, into three pieces. To be divided in such a way was not favourable from the point of view of the *feng shui*, he worried. His soul (if by any chance a crook like him possessed one) would have difficulty joining his ancestors, whom he had anyway never honoured.

"You are going to end up a ghost", he concluded, before rising above the town, its lights and its skyscrapers.

A ghost… This state, in fact, suited him well. He could, at his pleasure, torment the population until the end of time! He caught sight of the grandest of the buildings in Central, not far from the ferry terminals. He situated them more to the east in his memory, but this detail did not disturb him too much: the building in question, all in steel and glass, with an amazing clawed construction on top, he didn't remember at all. Long live development, and beautiful places to haunt! With a vigorous heave into the ether, he moved himself there.

*

Roger was the first to stand up again, dripping with blood. It was nothing, he knew it: scratches, superficial injuries. Siu Fung stood up as well. He held her tight against his chest. Surrounded by astonished passers-by they both cried. Near them, the tram, olive green and free of all commercial pollution, had come to a halt. The driver had come down onto the track and had cursed those demented people who were running along the rails and throwing firecrackers all over the place, when it wasn't even New Year.

"So which season is it, then?"

"The season of temperatures which make arrogant people ask stupid questions!" the man raged.

"OK, the season of temperatures which make

arrogant people ask stupid questions, but… of which year?" Siu Fung persisted.

Indifferent to the torrent of abuse which followed, she drew Roger towards the tram, to check if Johnny Kwok was underneath. They could see only a pair of burnt out shoes.

"It looks like it's he who has gone on a *voyage*", Chambon said.

They left the place, ignoring the driver's exhortations to wait with him until a representative of the forces of law and order arrived. A newspaper was blowing about on the pavement. Roger put his foot on it. The front page celebrated the first Chinese gold medal of the Olympic Games in Los Angeles, won by one Xu Hai-Feng, in the pistol-shooting.

"Do you think it's today's?" Siu Fung asked.

"It seems so."

"Great!" the girl commented soberly.

THE END

9 791092 475203